Truth Be Told

Michaela Austin

Preface

Some people say that everything happens for a reason, and fate decides life for us. Others say that there is no such thing as fate, and everything that happens has no rhyme or reason. I once believed the people who favored with fate. I mean, isn't it so easy to believe that bad things happen to lead us to greater things? We all need a little hope when things get tough. But when the bad things that occur throw you off track, you can't even progress to the good things that possibly lay ahead. This is why I now side with those of the people with enough common sense to say there is no reason... No rhyme. Maybe there is such thing as fate... I myself would like to believe I have a plan laid out for the future. But who's to say I do?

Chapter One.

My alarm rang. I rolled over on the cold floor and shut it off. I lay there for a while, listening to the icicles drip from the side of the house. I glanced out the window into the sunshine. I closed my eyes and let my mind wander.

I could hear my dad already awake and bringing in boxes from the car to unpack. His footsteps got closer and stopped outside of my door. I heard him set boxes down in the hallway, and walk away.

I stood up and stretched. Knowing I should help him, I pulled on a pair of jeans and a sweatshirt and trudged out to the car. I grabbed the last couple of boxes and brought them up to my room to unpack.

“I’ll be up soon with your bed,” Dad yelled to me from downstairs.

“Kay,”

I began to unpack the boxes, full of my crap. I noticed broken glass in the bottom of one of them, and went searching through the box to find the source. I pulled out a picture of my mom and I. The glass had broken from the frame. I was five years old in the picture, holding my mom's hand in front of my kindergarten classroom. My mom died three days after the picture was taken.

I had a weird feeling in the pit of my stomach. This was a sign.. I knew it. Something bad was going to happen in this house, but I had no idea what it was.

I could hear my dad struggling up the stairs with my bed. He walked in my room and set it down, then walked out as if he hadn't even seen me sitting on the floor in front of him.

He was so distant from the world, it wasn't even funny. My mom's death took a toll on all of us, but it hit him the hardest. He drastically went downhill, spiraling into denial and depression. I grew up with my grandparents; they raised me from the day my mom died until yesterday. I was seventeen now, growing up fast. I barely knew my own father. I wanted to get to know him, so he bought a new house in a small town called Barnesville, located in Maryland, with a population of 203 people. I moved to Barnesville with him, a huge change from San Diego, California. But I knew it would be worth the change as long as I could finally know my own father.

I put the picture back in the box as he brought up two more boxes.

"You going to get anything unpacked today?" He tried to make a joke, but failed.

I laughed anyway, trying to lighten the tense mood.

It didn't work; he walked away and left me by myself.

I sighed, and pulled out the broken picture of my mom and I.

If she were still alive, everything would've been so much simpler. I couldn't remember ever seeing my dad smiling. That scared me more than anything else. And my biggest fear? My biggest fear was that he would never be the same man again.

He was a good guy, he deserved to

be happy. There was no reason why he shouldn't have been. My mom passed away twelve years ago, long enough for him to at least fake a smile.

He was the only reason why I never wanted to fall in love. When you become so dependent on someone, how are you supposed to move on after they leave? Nothing would ever be the same without them, and that would never be worth the risk to me.

But maybe someday that guy would come along and surprise me. I had been waiting for that day since I was five, when I used to wait for Prince Charming to appear outside of my window with my mom by his side.

But I think who I was really looking for those many years ago, was my dad. I waited for us to be a family again, but those years were all wasted. They weren't wasted on fairytale dreams, and dreams of being a princess waiting for her prince to save her from the castle. They were wasted on dreams of having parents, dreams of having someone to look up to...

~

"Dinner will be ready in ten, it's steak. Do you like steak?"

I had been a vegetarian for six years now, but I nodded anyway. "Sounds good, I'll be right there."

He walked back downstairs, and I just watched the door as if my mom would appear in thin air in front of me.

Once I realized she wasn't going to, I unpacked another box and headed downstairs for dinner.

As I was walking down the spiral staircase, I heard the T.V. coming from the living room. Curious, I followed the voices from the news until I eventually found the living room. My dad was sitting in a recliner, eating his dinner.

He looked at me standing awkwardly in the doorway. "Are you going to get food?"

I nodded and walked out to the kitchen.

Steak, green beans, mashed

potatoes, and corn was sitting in plastic containers on the counter. I took one look at the steak, and thought I was going to throw up all over the kitchen. I opened the fridge, and saw lettuce and tomatoes. I made a quick salad, and walked back to the living room. I sat on the sofa and watched the news silently with my dad.

My mind was zoning out, until something on the news caught my attention and snapped me out of my trance.

"And in breaking news," The woman said loudly, "A mysterious death in Frederick has been ruled as a homicide. Police claim the victim, thirty-year-old Rita Harris, was stabbed to death in her home on St. Castle Street Friday night. We will be covering this story very closely and bringing you any updates."

I didn't have any idea why that got my attention, but I knew there was definitely a reason for it. I just had to figure it out.

~

"It's time to get up for school, Marcie." My dad's voice sounded crackly.

"Okay," I sighed into the darkness and got up.

Once I was dressed and ready for school, I sat in the living room and watched the news with my dad again.

"Breaking news from our full coverage in Frederick." My full attention was on the plastic looking woman on the T.V. "The homicide ruled death of Rita Harris is still being investigated, but Frederick police have involved the FBI. This morning, the chief of police gave us this statement,"

The chief of police came on T.V. "At this point in the case, we don't have any suspects, but we are looking into everyone who knew the woman. It appears as though she knew her killer. There was no sign of breaking and entering, but we believe she was strangled with a telephone cord. It's looking like we may have a serial killer on our hands, so we have involved the FBI as a precaution."

The Barbie lady appeared on the screen again. "So there you have it, a murder in the town of Frederick. We will be covering this story as closely as possible."

My dad's voice broke the silence. "Ready for school?"

Chapter Two.

I cautiously turned the key, and walked inside the dark house. My dad was working late, and I had stayed after school with my science teacher to catch up on schoolwork. I reached for the light switch on the wall.

Someone grabbed my hand. Before I could even scream, their other hand wrapped around my neck and squeezed.

I jolted upright, trying to catch my breath. I glanced around my empty room. I was sweating, and my breath was shallow. I lay back down, but my eyes refused to close.

Next thing I knew, I was at school. My dream haunted my every thought, my every move. People passed all around me, but it seemed as though I was standing still. Time seemed to pass without me, as it did when my mom first passed away. It felt as if I was holding on to the present by a thin string, hoping it would make me move forward. Maybe if I just cling tighter...

“Marcie. You alive?” Now I was home... How did I get home..?

“Yeah, I’m fine.”

“Well you passed out at school today. The nurse called me.” My dad’s voice was faint, almost as if it was filled with worry.

“I did?” My mind was going in so many different directions. “Maybe I just fell asleep... I didn’t sleep at all last night. That’s got to be it.”

“Maybe,” He shrugged. “Just get some rest.”

He walked away, and my eyes unwillingly closed.

~

There’s a story behind every face. Whether it’s what they ate for breakfast, or why they almost committed suicide last night. There’s a reason why every person is who he or she are. Something in their past made them that way, and there's nothing anyone can do to change them. Sometimes- well I've found most of the time- it's impossible to fix what is already broken.

My dad was one of those things. Nothing could ever fix him. He was broken, and the only one who could help him was my mom. But she wouldn't ever be there again. So he was broken, and that would never change.

But I wanted it to.

"Hi, is Sue busy?" Sue was my mom's old friend, who used to baby-sit me all the time when I was younger.

"Hold on one second dear," The receptionist mumbled into the phone.

"Hello?"

"Hi, Sue! This is Marcie."

"Marcie? No way! It can't be! How old are you now?"

"Seventeen." I laughed.

"Oh my stars! The last time I saw you, you were still a baby! What can I do for you Hun?"

"Well actually, I was hoping you still knew that woman Marisol."

"Well bless my soul, she has an

appointment in two hours! Why do you ask?"

"Is she still single and ready to mingle?"

Sue laughed. "Why yes she is! This isn't for your father by any chance, is it?"

"Maybe, maybe not." I laughed again. "Just tell her if she wants a real man, to be at The Jenks Corner Diner on Saturday night at nine."

"Will do, baby doll! Talk to you soon!" The line went dead.   I hung up the phone, feeling accomplished.

~

"Dad! Hurry up!"

"Hurrying," He called from in the bathroom.

I laughed. It was the night of his big date I set up with Sue's friend Marisol. I was definitely proud of myself for getting this far.

I would help him be happy again, no matter what. Even if it meant replacing mom.

Just as I was taking a sip of water,

dad walked out of the bathroom as if it was a catwalk, and posed.

I laughed so hard the water came out of my nose.

He was smiling, actually smiling. If my life could pause forever right here in this moment that would be okay with me.

“Ready?” I ask.

“You better believe it.” He beamed.

Chapter Three.

I woke up to the slamming of the back door. My heart stopped, and I froze. I felt as if I was glued to the couch. My breathing seemed way too loud for the silence of the house.

The lights turned on.

"Hey, kiddo. I thought you'd be up."

My heart started beating again, and I turned around to face him. "Oh my God. You scared the crap out of me."

He laughed. "Go to bed, you must be wiped out."

"I am!" I got up and started up the stairs.

"Marcie?"

I turned around to find myself face to face with my father's gleaming face. "Yeah, dad?"

"Thank you. You have finally made me happy again. And that's the nicest thing anyone has ever done for me. I love you, kiddo."

I smiled so big my cheeks hurt. "I love you too, dad."

~

"And in breaking news this morning, locals are shocked to learn that there are still no arrests in the murder of Rita Harris. But what they don't know? The Frederick police have no suspects yet." I could hear the Barbie lady's voice from the kitchen as I ate breakfast.

"Wow, police are awfully slow here." My dad noted.

"I was just thinking the same thing." I glanced at the clock. "Time for school," I sighed as I grabbed my bag and left.

I walked in the school and was almost immediately greeted by a guy in my Sociology class.

"Marcie!"

"Hey, Matt." I took a sip of my coffee and opened my locker.

"How are you on this lovely morning?"

"I'm good, you?"

"Great!" Matt said as he took my books from me.

"Thanks," I looked at Matt.

He smiled. Matt was perfect. He was on the football team, tall, tan, handsome, everything the head cheerleader wanted. But he was smart, and he didn't hide it. That was my favorite thing about him. His eyes sparkled.

"Hey, Marcie?"

I realized I was staring at him a moment too late. "Yeah, Matt?"

"I have to go to the football banquet Saturday, and I need a date. I was wondering if you wanted to go with me..." His words hung in the air like a noose.

"Oh! Uhm. I don't know... I'm not good at dating and relationships Matt..."

"I'll guide you through it Marcie. Just you and me. I'll do whatever it takes. From the first day you walked into Sociology and Mr. Kylie made you sit next to me, I knew you were the girl I wanted to be with for the rest of my life."

I was speechless.

"Marcie, don't make me get on my knees and beg you."

I still didn't say anything. It felt as though my words were caught in my throat.

Matt got on his knees and took my hand in his. "Marcie, will you pretty please be my girlfriend forever and ever?"

I laughed so hard I cried. Everyone was looking at me, waiting for my answer. "Yes, Matt. I will be your girlfriend forever and ever. Just don't give up on me."

Matt smiled. "I swear I won't." He stood up and kissed me.

And at that very moment, I realized I had broken the only rule I had set for myself: Don't fall in love.

~

Matt decided to drive me home so he could meet my dad. We walked in the door, and the only thing you could here was my dad snoring in the living room with the T.V. blasting.

"Do you want to go sit outside until he wakes up?"

Matt laughed a little. "Yeah, that sounds good."

We walked out to the backyard and lay in the grass.

Matt looked at me. "Is he going to like me?"

"You'll just have to find out for yourself."

He stuck his tongue out at me. "What about your mom? What's she like?"

I looked at the grass nervously. "My mom died when I was five."

"Oh, I'm so sorry Marcie." Matt leaned over and kissed my forehead.

"It's okay. You have to let go of people at some point."

He frowned. "I really like you, Marcie."

I smiled like a retarded penguin. "I like you too."

"I want you to meet my parents. My brother's birthday party is Friday night, please come."

"Okay," I smiled again.

I heard the back door open, and looked up to find my dad staring at us.

We stood up, and my dad stiffened.

"Dad, this is Matt. Matt, this is my dad." My voice sounded a little shaky.

They shook hands, my dad's piercing eyes never leaving Matt's face. "Come in and we'll all talk."

As we walked in the silent house, Matt looked at me with puzzled eyes.

I smiled, trying to lighten his mood and boost his confidence.

Dad disappeared into the kitchen, so I led Matt to the living room myself. I was turning down the T.V. as my dad walked in carrying drinks.

"Why'd you turn that down? I was waiting to hear about the homicide in Frederick." He said as he set the drinks on the coffee table.

"Sorry,"

He shook his head. "So Matt," He began.

Matt's shoulders tensed a little.

"What do you like to do?"

"Well," Matt breathed deeply. "I'm

on the football team, I play a little lacrosse, and I fish and hunt with my father on the weekends."

Dad nodded in approval. "Very good. And how are you doing in school?"

"3.957 GPA."

Dad's mouth drooped open a little. "Wow, impressive." He nodded.

Matt smirked.

"And Matt, I have to ask you this,"

All signs of a smile vanished from Matt's face. "What's that?"

"Why are you here with my daughter?"

Matt laughed a little. "Well, Mr. Tamblay, I really like your daughter."

"And what do you like about her?"

"Her personality. The way she lights up a room. Her laugh, her smile, the way her eyes shine when I look at her,"

I blushed.

"But most of all, the way she never let's anyone get in her way and tell her 'no you can't.' She's my best friend. And I respect her. There isn't one thing that I would change about her, she's absolutely perfect."

Dad nodded. "Would you like to stay for dinner?"

Matt let out a sigh of relief. "That sounds wonderful, thank you."

Dad got up and turned up the T.V. as the news came on. "I'll go start dinner." He left the room.

Matt moved closer next to me and wrapped his arms around me. "How was that?"

I smiled. "Perfect."

He kissed me, and I leaned my head on his shoulder as we watched the news.

Matt was telling me about yesterday's football practice when the Frederick investigation came on the news.

"And nothing new in the Frederick homicide of Rita Harris. The FBI claims they are dealing with an experienced serial killer, and are warning the locals to lock up their houses and take caution." The Barbie lady kept talking. "No suspects have been named in the case, but the police and the FBI have been doing their best to find the mastermind behind the tragic death of Harris."

"Marcie?" Matt was shaking me. "Marcie. What's wrong?" He glanced at the T.V., then back at me.

"Oh, I must have spaced out." I took a deep breath. "Sorry,"

"Are you sure you're okay, Marcie?"

"Yeah, just tired."

"Okay, I believe you." But the look on Matt's face said he didn't.

"Dinner's ready!" Dad yelled from the kitchen.

Matt stood up and wrapped his arm around my waist as if he thought I was going to fall over.

"Matt, I'm fine."

His arm didn't budge.

I sighed as we walked to the kitchen and sat down at the table.

Dad had cooked ham, steak, potatoes, and beans. Just one look and I thought I was going to throw up. I walked over to the fridge and took out lettuce, tomatoes, onions, and Italian dressing. I made a small salad and sat down at the table next to Matt.

"That's all you're eating?" Matt said with a mouth full of ham.

"Uhm, yeah. I'm a vegetarian."

Matt shook his head and laughed. "Being a vegetarian is for rich people who want to show off."

Dad laughed so hard milk came out of his nose.

I wanted to stay in this moment forever.

Chapter Four.

Some people say that once you've fallen in love, you've committed suicide. But what is that makes us scared to fall in love? Maybe it's the fact that you have given that person full power to destroy you. Just one word could completely break you, and once you give them that power, you can't take it back.

Or maybe it's the fact that once that person is gone, you'll never be the same. Everything reminds you of them. The way your clothes smell, the way you sleep at night, the sense of loneliness that doesn't leave you. Everything is them. They're gone, but somehow, they're everywhere and in everything.

This is what happened to my dad after my mom passed away. It was as if his heart shut down. He stopped doing what he loved to do because it reminded him of mom. He stopped performing, stopped working, stopped living. And I will never forget it.

"And still no arrests in the murder of Rita Harris," The T.V. was the only noise while dad and I ate breakfast. "Frederick police are second guessing themselves. They now believe that the murderer may not have had a personal relationship with Harris; the murder could have been spontaneous and random. Locals are starting to become anxious with the police and FBI, some say they have seriously thought about leaving the area until an arrest has been made. With the public going crazy, Frederick police have never been this pressured to solve a case. I'm Linda Seerly, reporting live in Frederick."

Dad finally broke the silence. "If people are thinking about leaving the area, why don't they just look for the killer themselves? People these days."

I laughed as I got up from the table and put my bowl in the sink. "Time for school, love you, dad."

"Love you too, kiddo."

I grabbed my bad and stepped outside to find Matt's car parked in the driveway. I smiled and slid into the passenger seat

~

"Don't forget, my brother's birthday party is tomorrow night." Matt reminded me as we walked in my front door.

"I know, Matt. How could I forget?" I smiled.

"Marcie... You forget a lot of stuff."

"Not important stuff," I teased.

He stuck his tongue out at me. "Yeah, Marcie, important stuff."

"Shut up," I pushed him playfully and kissed him.

He smiled. "Sociology homework time!"

"Please no."

"We have to! Do you want to pass senior year?"

"Yeah, I guess so."

"Good enough for me, get started."

"Fine," I grumbled as I pulled my binder out of my backpack.

Dad and Marisol walked into the house just as I sat down at the table.

"Marcie!" Marisol shrieked the moment she laid eyes on me. "You're so big! The last time I saw you, you were just a baby!"

I laughed and stood up to hug her. "It's nice to see you again, Marisol!"

"You too!" She looked over at Matt, who was quietly staring at his textbook. "Oh my, you even have a boyfriend!"

Matt finally looked up and smiled at Marisol. "Hi,"

"What's your name?"

Matt stood up and walked over to Marisol. "I'm Matt, it's nice to meet you."

Marisol looked impressed. "It's nice to meet you too, Matt! Awe, you guys are too cute together!"

Matt and I laughed.

"So are you and dad!" I beamed. "How are things with you two?"

Dad finally stepped into the conversation. "Well actually, that's what we're here to talk to you about."

"Oh?" So many things went

through my mind.

"Yes, let's go sit in the living room and talk."

"Okay," I said cautiously. I followed them into the living room, Matt tagging along behind me.

Dad and Marisol sat on the love seat together, and Matt and I sat across from them on the sofa.

I stared my dad down.

He looked at me with piercing eyes, and I knew I wasn't going to like what he had to say.

"Okay, dad. Spit it out."

Matt squeezed my hand, letting me know I was being too hard on him.

I tried to soften my stare as he shifted nervously.

"Well," He started. "Marisol and I have decided that we're ready to take our relationship more seriously."

"And what does that mean?"

Matt squeezed my hand again.

"Marisol is moving in with us until you graduate."

I eyed him suspiciously. "What's the catch, dad?"

"We're moving to Colorado May 28th."

"The day after graduation? Are you serious?"

"Unfortunately, yes." He looked sorry, but I wasn't buying it.

"That's pretty pathetic."

Matt didn't squeeze my hand.

"Well there's good news, too."

I laughed. "And what's that?"

"This house is fully paid for, and I would like to give it to you and Matt."

"Thank you sir," Matt said quietly before I could flip out.

"Yeah, thanks dad." I stood up and walked outside.

The fresh air was calming, and it wasn't long before I heard the door open and close behind me.

Matt sat down on the porch step beside me. "Marcie, he's just trying to make things easier on you."

"I haven't lived with my dad since I was five years old. We've lived together for a month now, and he already wants to leave me." I was crying now. "Why doesn't anyone stay with me?"

"Marcie, if your mom was given a choice, you know that she would be here with you right now. We both know that she wouldn't have traded you for the world. She loved you, and she had no choice."

I just looked at him.

"Marcie, you're never alone. She's always with you. She loved you, and you loved her. You both still love each other. You'll never be alone, Marcie, because she never left you."

I didn't know what to say. What do you say to someone who says exactly what you need them to say?

"Marcie, I love you. And I'll never leave you."

I smiled. "I love you, too." I whispered through tears.

"Like you said, you have to let go of people at some point." He said as he wrapped his arms around me.

"Thank you,"

"For what?"

"Being perfect,"

He laughed. "It's in my job description."

He was the only one I had ever met who could make me laugh when all I wanted to do was cry.

Chapter Five.

"Marcie, help Matt with Marisol's bags." Dad yelled to me from upstairs.

I stomped outside and grabbed some bags from her car.

Matt looked at me. "Marcie, you can't be unhappy. You have to let him go. Let him be happy."

I faked a smile and trudged inside. I set the boxes on the table and stared mindlessly out the window.

How could I let my dad go? I barely knew him as it was. He had just started being my father again, and he already wanted to quit. What had I done to make him give up on me so easily?

"Marcie?" Matt set more boxes on the table. "Baby you have to let him go." He tried to hug me, but I pushed him away.

"I'm sick of never being good enough for anyone."

Matt walked away.

~

"Still no arrest in the murder of Rita Harris, and the public is becoming restless. Police say that the only new update they have is that they now know that Harris was, in fact, strangled by a-" The woman's voice was cut off.

"Why do you people watch this bull anyway?" Marisol said in a nasally voice.

"It's the news."

"Yeah, well it's bull. None of it is real. It's society telling you lies. It's all lies!" She shrieked as she ran into the bedroom.

I looked at Matt. "She's psychotic, I swear."

"Don't be mean," He stuck his tongue out at me.

Dad poked his head in the doorway. "You need to apologize to her after dinner, Marcie. That was very rude." He disappeared back into the kitchen.

"Was I really that mean?"

Matt looked at his hands. "Kind of,"

I sighed grumpily and stood up. "Then I'll apologize." I slowly walked over to the bedroom door, and paused to knock.

I could hear Marisol talking extremely fast on the phone. "The body- At Mill Lake, don't suggest it."

I tried to listen more intently.

"No, I dumped the body Friday. It's all buried and everything." She laughed. "No one will ever find it!"

My heart stopped. A million thoughts ran through my head as I walked back into the living room.

"What's wrong?" Matt looked at me, puzzled.

"I just heard Marisol..."

"Did you apologize?"

I shook my head. "She was on the phone... Matt, she killed Rita Harris."

Matt stared at me for a moment. "Marcie. I understand that you hate her, and I understand why. But you can't lie about her committing a murder."

I sighed. "Come listen."

We tip toed to the bedroom door.

"-I already told you. I buried her body near Mill Lake. That woman is gone. No more worries about Harris."

Matt looked at me. His eyes were wide and his mouth was drooped open.

"I told you so,"

"Oh shit."

Chapter Six.

"Now what?" I whispered to Matt.

I could hear Marisol walking to the door.

Matt grabbed my wrist and ran. We were calmly sitting on the couch talking when Marisol walked out of her room.

She walked by the living room, and gave us a dirty look.

"We have to tell my dad," My heart was pounding in my chest.

Matt looked at me sympathetically. "It's going to crush him, Marcie." He scanned my face, looking for any trace of fear. "He might even kick you out."

I shook my head. "No, he-"

"Marcie, think about it." He cut me off. "You don't like Marisol. You don't want her to take your mom's place. I get that. But your dad doesn't. He's going to think you're trying to take away his happiness, and I know your dad. I don't think he would have any problem telling you to get out of his house."

I just stared at him. He was right. My dad was in love with Marisol.

When you're in love with someone, all of the bad is gone. You accept it, and pretend it will just go away if you leave it alone. But it doesn't. It builds up, until it's this wall that separates them from who you want them to be and who they are. He should've known better after what mom went through...

"Marcie, we have to go through this the right way."

"What's that?"

"Break the news to your dad one night when Marisol isn't around. He won't believe you. He'll tell you to pack your bags and get out. Don't make a scene. Just do it. But before you tell him, we'll record one of Marisol's phone calls. So after you leave, meet up with him for lunch the following day. Give him the recording."

"And you really think that's going to work?"

"Yeah. I do."

"But where will I go when he kicks me out?"

He looked at me for a moment, thinking. "Call me before you tell him. I'll be waiting for you outside, you can stay with me."

I nodded.

~

We crept inside as quietly as we could, trying not to tip Marisol off that we were home.

Matt pulled out the voice recorder from his backpack, and started crawling to the bedroom door. "Watch for your dad just in case he comes home early." He whispered.

I nodded.

Matt pressed his ear against the door and gave me a thumbs up.

Marisol was on the phone.

He took a deep breath and pressed

record.

~

"I'm going for it in ten." I whispered into my phone.

"Okay." Matt's voice was confident. "Marcie..."

"Yeah?"

"Be careful."

"I will." I hung up.

~

"Dad?" My crackly voice shook, breaking the long forgotten silence between us.

He looked up curiously. "Yes?"

"I need to tell you something. And you're probably not going to like it."

He put down his fork and knife, and looked up at me with piercing eyes. Beads of sweat dripped off his forehead.

I looked down at my plate of untouched chicken. "Well the other day," I took a deep breath. "I overheard Marisol talking on the phone."

He stared at me intently.

"And I think she may have some knowledge on that murder in Frederick." I stared into his hard eyes, waiting for his reaction.

"What are you trying to say?" He rested his head on his hands and stared into my eyes. They burned right through me.

"She killed Rita Harris, dad."

"You're absurd." He picked up his silverware and began to cut his meat.

"I may be a little crazy at times, I'm lazy, and sometimes a pain in the ass. But dad... I would never lie to you."

"Marcie, just shut that big mouth of yours."

"I know I may not be the perfect daughter," I continued. "And I may not be the daughter you wanted- maybe to short to be a sports star, not pretty enough to be a movie star, too heavy to be a supermodel, not enough confidence to be a pop star- but I know that I have done extremely well being the most loving daughter anyone has ever had. But you... You were never a father. And now you have this opportunity to be a great one," My voice was getting louder, no longer a whisper between the two of us. "And you're passing it up. You are giving up the first and last- the only- chance to be my father." I was yelling now. "Well I guess nothing has changed with you, has it?"

My dad stared at me, dumbfounded.

I stared back, confident.

"Marcie April..." He was at a loss for words, and I loved it.

"Yes, Shawn Robert?" I wasn't holding back one bit.

He took a deep breath. "Get out of my house."

"Will do." I got up from the table, went up to my room, and grabbed the bags Matt had helped me pack. I trudged down the spiral staircase and directly out the door.

Matt's truck was parked on the side of the road.

Chapter Seven.

"Hello?" My dad's voice was scratchy.

"Dad?"

He didn't answer me.

I sighed. "Dad, I know you're mad at me..." My eyes started to water. "And I understand why. I would be too. But you really need to listen to me. Just give me one chance to prove it to you..."

Silence. After a moment, his crackly voice returned. "How?"

"Well I was hoping you could meet me for lunch..."

"Where?" His voice was stiff, as if it was a chore.

"The Market Grill?"

"Time?"

"One."

"Don't waste my time, Marcie."

"I won't let you down, dad."

The line went dead.

I stared at my cell phone, bewildered.

Matt woke up next to me.

"Hey, early bird."

I looked at him for a moment. "I called him."

"How'd it go?"

"Okay, I guess."

"It's only going to get better, Marcie."

"I know,"

~

I stared mindlessly out the big window next to my seat. The straw paper I was twisting broke, and I couldn't help but wonder if that was a sign.

Before I could give it too much thought, my dad slid into the seat across from me.

"You couldn't have gotten anything

else for a table? You know I don't like booths..." He mumbled.

"No dad, actually I don't."

He stared at me coldly. "Well where's this proof?"

I dug the voice recorder out of my purse and set it on the table in front of him.

"What's this?"

I sighed. "A voice recorder, dad. Put the headphone in your ear and press play."

He did as I said.

Marisol's voice echoed in my head as I witnessed my dad's heart break.

He shut the voice recorder off and pushed it across the table to me. "We need to go." His voice was almost inaudible.

~

I had no idea where we were going, and I didn't ask. My dad was silent as he drove through town. He finally pulled over.

I glanced out the window to find

myself face to face with the police station.

"Dad," I looked at his pale face and took in every detail. "Why are we here?"

He looked down, avoiding my eyes. "I believe you, Marcie. And I'm so sorry..." He started crying hysterically.

"It's okay... Love is blind. You couldn't have helped it even if you wanted to." I hugged him awkwardly as he cried.

After a moment he sat up, dried his eyes, and looked at me. "I am so sorry... Please come back home, Marcie."

"I will."

"Well let's go bust this bitch."

~

"Would you shut that stupid news off already?" Marisol nagged from the kitchen.

"Okay Marisol, sorry." I shut the TV off and walked into the kitchen.

Marisol was sitting at the table writing in a journal.

I couldn't help but giggle at her

ignorance.

"Now what's so funny? Gosh, you're so stupid Marcie." She looked up at me with a disgusted look on her face.

"Maybe, but I will always look down on you. And you'll always look up at me."

Marisol stood up and stared at me. "All you are is a piece of white trash." She laughed in my face. "No one will look up to you. You'll never amount to anything." She laughed again, then sat back down and resumed writing.

There was a knock at the door.

I smiled to myself as I walked over to the door and opened it.

"Is Marisol Garichey here?" Officer Randolph asked me.

"Why yes she is," I smiled even wider. "Hey Mar, someone's here for you."

I sat down at the table as Marisol walked to the door.

She took one look at Officer Randolph, and I could tell she wasn't going to make it easy on him. She turned around and ran upstairs as fast as she could. But she wasn't fast enough.

Officer Randolph grabbed her wrist and yanked her back down the stairs.

I could hear the handcuffs click as he locked them on her wrists.

"Marisol Garichey, you are under arrest for the murder of Rita Harris. You have the right to remain silent. Anything you say can, and will be used against you in a court of law. You have the right to an attorney. If you cannot afford an attorney, one will be appointed to you by the state."

And Marisol was gone.

Chapter Eight.

"Breaking news in the town of Frederick as an arrest in the murder of Rita Harris has been made." My dad and I glued our eyes to the Barbie lady talking on the TV. "Police arrested forty-two year old Marisol Garichey earlier today. Garichey was residing with her former boyfriend and his daughter, Shawn and Marcie Tamblay." We looked at each other sympathetically.

"Marcie, I was wrong for letting her tear us apart so quickly..."

"Dad, it's okay."

He smiled at me. "I'm going to bed, kiddo. See you in the morning. Love you."

"Love you too, dad."

~

"Marcie! You need to get up right now!" My dad's voice sounded worried.

"Why, what's wrong?"

"You need to come down stairs. Get dressed." He flitted out of the room.

I glanced at the clock. It blinked 1:58. I got up and pulled on jeans and a sweatshirt. I ran down the stairs as fast as I could. "Dad, what's-" The fire trucks and ambulances answered my question. "What happened?" I breathed.

"I'm not sure. But they just carried Mr. Johnson out of his house on a stretcher."

"Oh my gosh,"

"Go turn on the news, kiddo."

I nodded and frantically ran to the living room. I turned on the TV, and sure enough, there was Barbie lady.

"We are following breaking news in Barnesville this morning, where family members found thirty-three year old

Isaac Johnson dead in his home."

I stared at the TV, shocked.

"Police arrived at the scene after Johnson's sister, Mindy Carwell, called 911. Carwell had arrived at Johnson's around 1:00 this morning after attending a concert nearby. She claims that Johnson was expecting her, and knew she would be arriving this late. Carwell claims that the door was unlocked, and when she stepped inside, she found Johnson in the kitchen strangled to death."

Images of Mr. Johnson's house appeared on the TV.

"Police say that this murder is very similar to the recent murder of Rita Harris, but when asked about the possibility of arresting an innocent woman, the police refuse to believe that was possible. We will be following this homicide ruled case very closely, and bringing you any new details."

"Uhm, dad. You might want to come look at this."

Dad walked into the living room and slumped into his recliner.

I watched as his eyes slowly processed the headline.

"Murder in Barnesville?" He seemed puzzled.

"Mr. Johnson was murdered, dad."

~

"Marcie, the case is on!" Dad yelled to me from the living room.

I grabbed my plate of salad and rushed to the couch.

"Mysteries in two recent murder cases still haunt the state of Maryland."

My dad looked over at me with a puzzled expression.

I shrugged.

"After Isaac Johnson was found strangled in his Barnesville home early this morning, police and FBI officers began to question the similarities of the murder of Rita Harris. Harris was found in her Frederick home, strangled by a phone cord, which is also the case with Johnson. Police have now decided to release Marisol Garichey, who was arrested yesterday for Harris's murder."

My jaw dropped.

"Frederick police and the FBI both believe that arresting Garichey was a mistake, and they have arrested the wrong person. We will be reporting any breaking news in these related cases."

"I can't believe it..." Dad was speechless. "I have to call her, and apologize.."

"So do I..."

I ran up to my room and dialed Matt's number.

"Hello?" Just the sound of his voice relaxed me.

"It wasn't Marisol." My voice trembled.

"What did you say?"

"Marisol didn't kill Rita Harris."

"Then what was she talking about when she said she 'got rid of Harris'?"

"I don't know, but the police let her go."

I could tell Matt was getting irritated. "What's going on?"

"Come over and see for yourself."

"I'll be there in ten."

"Okay,"

"Love you, Marcie."

"I love you too." I hung up.

I decided to change, and then rushed downstairs to find myself face to face with Marisol.

She looked at me as if she was disgusted.

"Marisol... I am so sorry. For everything."

"Save it." She said the words as if they were garbage in her mouth.

"I mean it, Marisol. I should have embraced my dad's new found happiness. But I didn't, I ruined it instead. And I really am sincerely sorry."

She didn't say anything for a moment, just sighed. "I forgive you, Marcie."

I looked over at my dad to see a smile written across his face as if it never left.

"But I also have some apologies to you, Marcie."

I looked at her, puzzled.

"I haven't been treating you very nicely, and I should've been from the very start. I mean, after all, you are the only reason why I am this happy. If it weren't for you being such a good daughter, I would've never had the chance to be a better person."

I smiled. "Well, I forgive you. And thank you. But I do have one question for you,"

"Anything." Marisol gleamed back at me.

"What were you talking about on the phone? Something about how you 'got rid of Harris'..?"

She laughed to herself. "Oh my gosh, Harris was my dog! She died last week, and I buried her at Mill Lake, where we used to go every Summer."

"Oh my gosh," I couldn't help but laugh along with her. "Well that's a whole different story!"

My dad chimed in with our laughter.

We were interrupted by a knock at the door.

"That's probably Matt," I said as I opened the door.

"Hey." Matt stepped inside. "So are you going to tell me what's going on?"

I sighed. "Yeah. Let's go watch the news."

Matt looked confused, but followed me to the living room anyway.

The news was already on, and the Barbie lady was going over new stories.

"And breaking news in the Harris murder and the Johnson Murder. The FBI has confirmed that the two cases are very much related, and most likely have the same killer."

Matt looked at me.

"Rita Harris was found in her Frederick home early last week, strangled to death by her phone cord. Isaac Johnson was found in his Barnesville home early this morning, strangled by his phone cord. There have been no other discoveries on either case, but we will be bringing you any new updates."

"Isaac was killed?" Matt sounded confused.

"This morning." My dad answered him in his raspy voice.

"Isaac your neighbor?"

Dad nodded.

"Oh my gosh..."

No one spoke for a moment, no one dared to.

"Well," Marisol broke the silence. "I'm going to bed."

"Me too, and Matt you're welcome to sleep on the couch tonight." Dad mumbled.

"Alright, thank you Mr. Tamblay."

Dad nodded, and followed Marisol into their bedroom.

"I'll get you some blankets," I said as I stood up. I cautiously walked into the hallway and opened the closet door. I grabbed three blankets and rushed back to the living room. "Here," I set them on the couch next to him.

Matt turned to face me. "I love you, Marcie."

I smiled. "I love you too,"

He kissed my cheek. "You look exhausted, go to bed."

I shook my head.

"Then cuddle with me," He smiled.

I gleamed back at him. "Okay,"

Matt stood up and laid two of the blankets out on the floor. He laid down on them and smiled at me.

I laid down next to him, and he covered us up with the last blanket.

I fell asleep within minutes, listening to his heart beat.

Chapter Nine.

I woke up to footsteps in the kitchen. They were loud, as if it was someone with heavy boots on. I figured they were my dad's, and decided to ignore them and go back to sleep. After a moment, I heard the boots go up the stairs. My dad knew I wasn't up there...

"Matt?" I shook Matt, trying to wake him up as quietly as possible. "Matt, wake up!" I was almost in tears now. I could hear the boots getting closer to the top of the stairs... "Matt!"

"Marcie?" Matt sat up. "What's wrong?"

"Be quiet." I listened for a moment,

trying to tell if the person upstairs heard us. They were still walking around. "Someone's upstairs. It's not you, it's not me, it's not my dad, it's not Marisol."

Matt stopped breathing for a moment. "Go crawl into their bedroom and wake your dad up. I'm going upstairs."

I clung to Matt's shirt. "I don't want you to..."

"Marcie, I have to. Go get your dad. We don't have much time."

I nodded. "Be careful. I love you," I kissed Matt, and crawled to dad's bedroom.

The door was already open, so I crawled over to his side of the bed.

"Dad,"

"Marcie? Is that you?"

I could hear Matt going up the stairs, and I wanted to throw up. "Someone's in the house, dad. Matt just went upstairs to find them. Please go help him, daddy."

Dad jumped out of bed, and sprinted up the stairs.

I decided to wake Marisol up, and

crawled over to her side of the bed. "Marisol?"

"Marcie?" Marisol opened her eyes.

"Someone's in the house. Dad and Matt are upstairs trying to find them."

"Oh my gosh..." Marisol paused for a moment, and looked at me with a fake smile. "It's going to be okay, Marcie."

I nodded.

There was running upstairs.

I ran out to the kitchen just in time to see a man dressed in black wearing a black ski mask run down the stairs and out the door.

Matt and dad ran down the stairs not far behind the man.

"Is he gone?" Dad was breathless, and could barely talk.

I nodded.

"There's your murderer right there." Matt said as he shut and locked the door. "Not a doubt in my mind. And whoever they were, they were after you, Marcie." Matt looked at me with soft eyes.

I walked slowly back the living room and collapsed onto the blankets. I heard dad's bedroom door shut, and Matt laid down next to me.

"Hey." He whispered in my ear. "Marcie, are you okay?" He wrapped his arms around me.

I clutched his shirt. "Yeah," I breathed.

Matt held me as tight as he could without squishing me. "I'll never let go."

My eyes closed, and his heart beat was the only noise in the empty house.

~

"The police refuse to do anything!" Dad slammed the door behind him and slumped into a chair. "A wanted murderer came into our house, and they won't do anything?! They're probably involved! Fine, we'll find the murderer ourselves."

"Let's do it." Matt sat in the chair across from him.

"How about no." I said firmly.

"Marcie, it's either that or they keep trying to kill you." Matt glared into my eyes. "I don't think he's going to give up until he kills you."

I looked down at my feet.

"Yeah, Matt's right Marcie."

I sighed.

"Wouldn't surprise me if he came back tonight." Matt said.

"Yeah, me either." Dad agreed.

I walked into the living room and sat on the couch next to Marisol.

"They're ridiculous."

I nodded in agreement.

~

"Okay. Marcie, all you have to do is exactly what you did last night. Wake Matt and I up, and we'll get him." Dad whispered from his bedroom door.

I nodded and shut off the light.

Matt spread the blankets out and laid down.

I followed him, and he covered us up. I clutched his shirt again, scared of the night to come. I closed my eyes and forced myself to sleep.

A few hours later, I woke up to the sound of heavy boots yet again. I squeezed my eyes shut and wished it was all a bad dream. But I knew it wasn't. I heard footsteps go up the stairs.

I shook Matt, and he was instantly in action.

I crawled over to dad's room and shook him. He was ready. He woke up Marisol.

Matt and dad stood in the hallway outside of the kitchen, out of sight.

I went into the kitchen and made as much noise as possible. I opened cabinets, took out glasses, and poured water into a glass.

It wasn't long before I could hear faint footsteps coming down the stairs.

I turned my back to the foot of the staircase, and waited.

The footsteps got closer, I could hear them right behind me.

I didn't dare turn around.

They got closer, and then stopped. The only noise in the house was my shallow breaths.

A hand wrapped around my mouth, and my breathing stopped.

"Don't fight, and I'll make this as painless as possible." The voice sounded familiar, but not a voice I could pair with someone I knew. The murderer walked over to the phone. Big mistake turning his back against the hallway.

Dad and Matt leaped into the kitchen, bringing the murderer to the ground, with me following him.

I hit the linoleum and it felt as if I shattered into pieces. There was a piercing pain in my side. I stared at the ceiling, waiting for the end.

Dad and Matt struggled to get the murderer down.

Marisol came running into the kitchen.

I watched as dad and Matt shoved him around.

"Let's see who you really are." Matt said as he pulled off the black ski mask.

And as soon as it was off, my life stopped. Such a familiar voice, but didn't match anyone I knew. Until now.

I watched my dad's face as his heart was once again torn into pieces.

Tears filled his eyes.

Marisol rushed over to me and held me in her arms.

Dad fell to the floor on his knees. "Brenda?"

My mother's face turned away from us. "Shawn,"

"Mom?" I breathed.

"Don't ever call me that." Her cold, hard eyes returned to my face as she looked me over.

Matt looked at me with worry and longing.

And in that split second, she was gone.

My mother pushed Matt down and ran.

~

"Where are we going?"

"It's a surprise." The sunshine brightened Matt's face as he drove through the dull state of Maryland.

"Are we almost there?"

"Look out your window," Matt smiled.

I looked, and sure enough I was

staring at Washington Dulles International Airport. "Oh my gosh! San Diego?!"

Matt nodded. "You got it, babe." His smile gleamed in the sunshine. "We come back tomorrow night, but I figured it would be good to go see other family."

"Thank you," I leaned over and kissed his cheek.

"Your welcome."

Chapter Ten.

"Well bless my soul!" Gram exclaimed as we greeted them in the airport lobby. "You look so grown up Marcie! And look at this fine young gentleman!" Gram looked Matt up and down, and winked at me.

I laughed. "I missed you guys!" I hugged her and Gramps. "Guys, this is Matt, my boyfriend."

Gram smiled and shook his hand. "It's so nice to meet you!" She hugged him as tight as she could.

"Hey," Gramps said as he firmly shook Matt's hand.

Matt smiled at both of them.

"Do you really have to leave tonight?" Gram's voice was full of excitement and sadness.

I nodded. "Unfortunately, yeah. I have to get back to dad."

Gram nodded. "I understand."

~

"Shut the door, Marcie. It's late. And don't forget to lock it." Matt whispered as we walked in the door to my dad's house in Maryland.

"They're probably waiting up for us. They knew we were coming back this late."

"Well there's no lights on." Matt turned on the kitchen lights to reveal my worst nightmare.

Marisol laid on the floor by the telephone, the cord wrapped around her neck. My dad was laid out next to her, still breathing raspy, shallow breaths.

"She's still-" My dad gasped for air. "Upstairs-"

Matt ran up the stairs.

A woman in all black ran down the stairs just as fast as Matt had ran up them.

"Matt! She's gone."

Matt walked down the stairs, defeated. "Call 911."

~

"Dad?"

He slowly opened his eyes and looked around the room. "Where am I?" He mumbled.

I sighed. "In the hospital, dad."

"Oh. Yeah. I forgot for a second there." He glanced around the room again, taking it all in. He sighed.

"I'm going to the police station with Matt in a second."

Dad nodded.

"They might need to ask you some questions..."

"I know," He nodded again.

Matt walked in the room. "Hey, Mr.

T! How are you feeling?"

Dad shrugged. "Alright, I suppose."

Matt nodded, then looked at me. "Ready to go?"

"Oh yeah." I breathed.

~

"I'm sorry but we can't help you. If you come here again we're going to have to report you and help you get psychiatric help."

"But she's alive! I've seen her with my own eyes!"

The woman police officer rolled her eyes. "Miss, you need to leave."

"No, you will listen to me because I'm-" I struggled against Matt as he dragged me out of the police station.

"Marcie, stop." Matt looked at me, his eyes hard and piercing.

I shut my mouth and followed him out to the car. "We'll figure something out. Until then, you can stay at my house."

I nodded. "Go to my dad's so I can get my stuff, please."

"Okay," Matt said. His eyes never moved from the road, and he didn't say anything.

I stared out the window and suddenly found myself back at my dad's. "I'll just be a second." I mumbled as I climbed out of Matt's car with him right behind me. I fumbled to get my key in the lock.

Matt swung the door open and took a step inside. "Someone's been here."

I stepped inside next to him and took in the room.

The kitchen table and chairs were all over the floor, food everywhere, the knives thrown at the walls.

I walked over to the knives.

Written in blood on the wall, it said "Watch your back, bitch."

I sighed. "It was her."

"I know." He paused, trying to fit words together, but knowing they wouldn't sound the way he wanted them to. "I'll go check the damage upstairs and grab your things. Go wait in the car." He trudged up the stairs, wasting no time at all.

I took one last look at the blood on the wall, and walked out to the car silently. "We have to make a quick stop on the way to my house." Matt said as he put my bags in the back seat. He climbed into the front seat and started the car.

I watched the house fade through the window as Matt drove down the driveway, and it was gone. Everything was gone.

When the life you just got used to gets taken away from you, how are you supposed to make a new one? When the person you're supposed to be gets torn down, who are you expected to be? How could anyone expect you to recover from something so tragic? Everything -and everyone- is different. No one is who they say they are. They promise to be this person who never leaves you. This person who is there, every step, stumble, and jump of the way.

But they disappear. They change, and the promises they once made mean nothing anymore. Who they were, and who they are become two completely separate people. And nothing is more heart-wrenching than watching the people you have leaned on through everything, change into someone you never expected them to be.

Of course I've learned that nothing stays the same. But it's funny how everything never seems to change until you see it.

Your eyes start to burn when you look at them. Your heart drops into your stomach. and your temper goes up with every move they make. And even though it might seem as if you're mad at them, you're hurt. So hurt, that you don't even think of it as pain.

~

I looked out the window as we pulled into an unfamiliar driveway.

"I'll be right back." Matt got out of the car and walked up to the door. He knocked, then stood on the steps waiting for an answer.

A man answered the door. The minute he saw Matt, he threw his arms up in the air and gave him a huge hug.

Matt pointed to the car, explaining something to the man.

I peered out the window, trying to piece together Matt's mind.

Matt started walking back to the car. "Marcie, come here. I want you to meet someone."

I got out of the car and clutched Matt's hand as we walked back over to the man.

"Marcie, this is Todd, my uncle." He looked at Todd. "This is my girlfriend, Marcie."

I smiled. "Hi," I said as I shook his hand.

Todd smiled in return.

"Marcie, Todd is an FBI officer. He agreed to help us track down your mother."

I nodded. "Thank you so much..."

"It's not a problem, Marcie. I've heard so many wonderful things about you, and it's an honor to help someone who makes Matt so happy." Todd smiled.

"Thank you," I whispered.

Todd nodded. "Well you two can go relax and all of that, but tomorrow I'm going to have to steal Matt from you, Marcie."

I laughed. "Okay, I'll make it without getting killed."

Matt and Todd laughed along with my dry humor.

~

"Bye, Marcie. I'll be back no later than four. I love you!"

"Wait, I'm coming." I slowly crawled out of bed and slumped over to Matt's kitchen.

He smiled at my bed head and plain face.

"I love you," I whispered as I lightly kissed his cheek. "Be home soon, I miss you already."

Matt's smile grew bigger. "I love you too, Marcie. Be good." He kissed my cheek, and was gone.

I walked back into the bedroom

and got dressed.

Chapter Eleven.

Dad's face lit up as I walked into the tiny hospital room. "Hey, kiddo."

"Hey, dad." I smiled. "How are ya?"

He laughed. "Still can't feed myself or do my business alone, so how do you think?"

I shrugged. "Sounds good to me."

A smile spread across his face. "I miss you, kiddo."

"I miss you too, dad." I smiled back at him, holding back the tears that were welling up behind my soft green eyes. "I have to go, but Matt and I will be back to eat dinner with you. We want to watch you suffer because you can't feed yourself." I stuck my tongue out at him.

He laughed. "Thanks so much."

"Anytime," I smiled wider. "I love you."

"I love you too, Marcie."

I wiped tears from my eyes as I walked out to Matt's car. I got in and started it. I listened to the soft noise of the engine as I allowed a few tears to flow over the edges of my eyes. I wiped them away and held my breath as I pulled out of the hospital parking lot.

I watched the trees pass me by as I made the five minute journey back to Matt's house.

Life seemed to pass me by lately. Everything was held back, waiting for me to catch up. But I was running out of breath and time. It was almost as if there was a timer in my head; every second that went by left a soft 'tick' in my head that echoed through my brain.

I pulled into the driveway and got out of Matt's car. I dug for the house key he gave me in the bottom of my purse. I unlocked the door, and cautiously stepped inside.

Part of me expected to see the furniture tipped over, everything thrown around the house, and blood on the walls.

But there was nothing wrong. Matt's shirt still hung over the back of the chair in the living room, his shoes still sat next to the door in the kitchen. There was no presence of anyone else here but me.

I could smell Matt. Matt lingered everywhere in this house, and I longed for him to be here standing next to me, holding my hand.

I sat my purse on the kitchen table and walked into the bedroom. I quickly made Matt's bed and walked back into the kitchen. I turned my back to the door as I looked through the fridge.

I could here footsteps outside on the porch. "Finally," I whispered to myself as Matt opened the door and stepped inside. "You're back already?" I said without looking in his direction.

His footsteps stopped behind me

and his arms wrapped around my shoulders.

I turned around to face him, to look into his chocolate brown eyes.

My mother's beady black eyes met mine.

I gasped as her hand wrapped around my mouth, the other clutching my neck. I pushed her to the ground and started to run to the door.

Her legs wrapped around mine.

My head hit Matt's oak wood floor, and I felt myself walk the thin line between consciousness and unconsciousness. I forced my eyes open as my mother grabbed a butchering knife from the counter.

She kneeled over me as she unsuccessfully tried to drive the knife into my chest.

I realized just how strong she was as I fought to keep the knife a safe distance from my heaving body.

And in those last moments, every faint memory of my mother played through my mind before it drifted away.

And for the first time in my life, I

wished she was dead. I wanted more than anything for her to be dead.

I had spent almost thirteen years of my life wanting my mother to talk to me again, wanting her to hold me again.

And there she was, trying to kill me.

The knife was at my throat. I could feel the blade against my cool skin.

I looked at her. I looked in her eyes, looking for fear, guilt, remorse. And the only thing that stared back at me was hate.

The knife pushed on my skin.

I heard the door open as my eyes closed.

There was yelling coming from somewhere.

I felt relief from something, and someone was holding me. I opened my eyes.

Matt's eyes looked into mine as tears fell from his eyes. "You're okay, Marcie." He breathed deeply and nodded, agreeing with himself. "You're okay."

I closed my eyes again as more

footsteps entered the room.

"Marcie?"

I opened my eyes.

"I love you," Matt kissed my cheek and carried me into the bedroom. "It's okay, you're okay."

"I know," I nodded. "I love you, too." I closed my eyes again, and crossed the line of unconsciousness.

10 Years Later.

"Mommy, look at me!"

I look into the eyes of my three year old daughter who is the spitting image of Matt. She's wearing my high heels and my purse is around her shoulder. I scoop her up into my arms as she giggles.

"I love you, momma!"

"I love you too, Mia." I smile and squeeze her little body.

Matt walks into the kitchen and hugs us.

"Momma, what's that mark from?" Mia's little hand brushes against my throat, lingering on my scar.

I shook my head. "I don't know, Mia."

Matt looks at me, and takes Mia from my arms. "Time for bed," Matt says as he chases her into her bedroom.

~

Matt's cool hand lingers on my throat. He caresses my scar and looks me in the eyes. "You're perfect." He whispers.

I swallow hard, holding back tears.

"Don't ever forget it." He kisses my scar.

And in that moment, I realize that I don't regret anything.

Some people say that everything happens for a reason, and fate decides life for us. Others say that there is no such thing as fate, and everything that happens has no rhyme or reason. I once believed the people who said there was no fate. I mean, isn't it so easy to believe that bad things happen because you deserve them? We all lose a little hope in our journeys through life. But when great things happen for no reason at all when you don't deserve them, you have to believe there is a reason. This is why I now side with those of the people with enough faith to say there is a reason... A rhyme. Maybe there is no such thing as fate... I myself would like to believe I have earned the good in my life- a beautiful daughter, a perfect husband, and a healthy father- but who's to say I have?

www.ingramcontent.com/pod-product-compliance
Ingram Content Group UK Ltd.
Pitfield, Milton Keynes, MK11 3LW, UK
UKHW041925190726
13854UKWH00003B/1457

9 781105 661006